The Robin Family

René Robinette

Houghton Mifflin Company   Boston   1989

To Dave

Library of Congress Cataloging-in-Publication Data

Robinette, René.
☐ The Robin Family

☐ Summary: Four silly adventures of the irrepressible
   Robin family – Mom, Dad, Chelsea, and Taylor.
   [1. Family life – Fiction. 2. Humourous stories]
   I. Title
   PZ7.R554R. 1989   [E]   88-32833
   ISBN 0-395-49214-9

Printed in the United States of America

Y   10 9 8 7 6 5 4 3 2 1

The Robin Family

Everyone in the Robin family was mad.

Mrs. Robin was mad because her tongue was sticking out and she couldn't get it back in.

Mr. Robin was mad because he had a runny nose on both sides.

Chelsea Robin was mad because her tongue was sticking out, she had a runny nose on both sides, and her hair was messy.

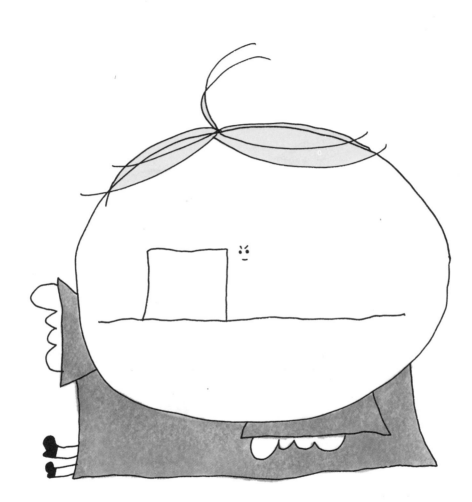

Taylor Robin was mad because her first tooth finally grew in and it was too big.

What could the Robin family do?

Mrs. Robin put some jelly on her tongue, which made it slippery, and it slipped right back into her mouth.

Mr. Robin put a Band-Aid on his nose, which made it stop running.

Chelsea Robin put some jelly on her tongue,
put a Band-Aid on her nose, and hung upside down on the couch,
which straightened her hair out.

But Taylor Robin had to wait until her mouth got big enough
to fit her tooth.

She stayed mad about that until Chelsea put jelly on her tooth. That made it taste good.

Grumpy Baby

Mrs. Robin and Chelsea were folding clothes when they heard Taylor in her room.
"She woke up early," said Mrs. Robin.
"I hope she isn't grumpy."

When Chelsea opened the door to Taylor's room, she couldn't believe what she saw. Taylor woke up more than grumpy — she woke up a gorilla!

Chelsea quickly left and shut the door.

Horrible noises came from Taylor's room.
CRASH! BANG! ARRAUGH!
Chelsea ran to get Mrs. Robin.

But Mrs. Robin was on the phone, so Chelsea waved her arms around and tried to look like Taylor.

Mrs. Robin said, "Not now, Chelsea, I'm on the phone."

Chelsea was worried that Taylor would never turn back into a real baby.

She was relieved when Mrs. Robin finally got off the phone.
At Taylor's door Mrs. Robin said, in her sweetest voice,
"Taylor, do you want to snuggle with Mommie?"
Chelsea watched as Mrs. Robin's words fell, like magic,
through the door.

When they opened the door, there was Taylor, looking more like herself. The magic in Mrs. Robin's words had turned her back into a real baby.

Beef Surprise

One day Mrs. Robin made a special meal. She called it Beef
Surprise. She spent all day preparing it and was
excited when it was done.

When Mrs. Robin put her meal on the table, Mr. Robin said,
"I'm so hungry I could eat anything."
"Even snails from the back yard?" Chelsea wondered.

Mrs. Robin was the first to try Beef Surprise. She took a big bite, smiled proudly, and said, "Yum! Isn't this good!"

But when Mr. Robin took a bite, he gagged.
He looked like he had just eaten snails.

Chelsea took one bite, dropped her fork, and said,
"Yuck! This tastes awful!"

Taylor didn't say anything. She was squeezing peas between her fingers and watching them fly into the mashed potatoes.

Mrs. Robin began to cry.

Then Mr. Robin had an idea.

He got some ketchup and poured it over their Beef Surprise.

The ketchup tasted good, and they all ate their food.

33

When they finished eating, Mrs. Robin dried her eyes and said, "The *next* time I make Beef Surprise I'll use lots and lots of ketchup."

When they heard that they would have to eat Beef Surprise again, Mr. Robin, Chelsea, and Taylor gasped.
They looked like they had just eaten snails.

Growing Up

While walking home from school one day, Chelsea looked down at her hands and thought that they seemed bigger than usual. She began to worry.

Chelsea quit worrying when she decided that her hands were
just swollen. After a good night's rest, they would look
normal again.

But the next morning Chelsea's hands looked even bigger. They were so big that she couldn't hold a spoon to eat her cereal. And when she gave Taylor a hug, she needed only one hand to hug Taylor's whole body.

By lunch Chelsea's hands were so big she couldn't put her sweater on. By dinner they were so big she couldn't scoot her chair up to the table.

Chelsea felt sick. She went to her room and got into bed.
She hid her hands under the blanket.

Mr. and Mrs. Robin could tell something was bothering Chelsea.
"Look at my hands!" she cried, and waited for their screams.

"Your hands look okay to me," said Mrs. Robin.
"Chelsea, you're just growing up," said Mr. Robin.
"Oh," said Chelsea.

44

Chelsea wanted to see for herself, so she went to stand in front of the mirror.

"EEEEEEEK!"